E $12.95
La   Langoulant, Allan
             Everybody's
           different

DATE DUE

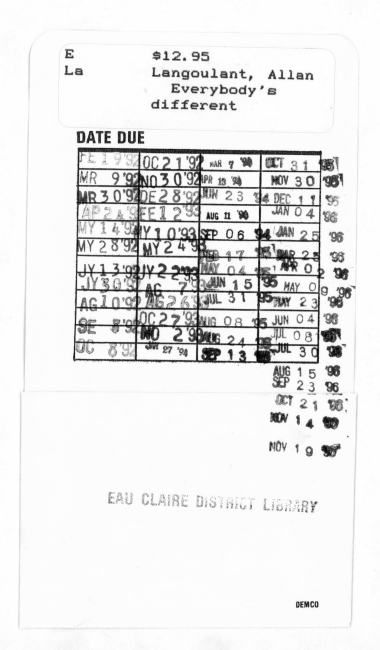

FE 19 '92	OC 21 '92	MAR 7 '90	OCT 31 '95
MR 9 '92	NO 30 '92	APR 13 '94	NOV 30 '95
MR 30 '92	DE 28 '92	JUN 23 '94	DEC 11 '95
AP 24 '92	FE 12 '93	AUG 11 '90	JAN 04 '96
MY 14 '92	MY 10 '93	SEP 06 '94	JAN 25 '96
MY 28 '92	MY 24 '93	FEB 17 '95	MAR 23 '96
JY 13 '92	JY 22 '93	MAY 04 '95	APR 02 '96
JY 30 '92	AG 7 '93	JUN 15 '95	MAY 09 '96
AG 10 '92	AG 26 '93	JUL 31 '95	MAY 23 '96
SE 8 '92	OC 27 '93	AUG 08 '95	JUN 04 '96
SE 8 '92	NO 2 '93	AUG 24 '95	JUL 08 '96
OC 8 '92	JUN 27 '94	SEP 13 '95	JUL 30 '96

AUG 15 '96
SEP 23 '96
OCT 21 '96
NOV 14 '96
NOV 19 '96

DEMCO

Everybody's Different

For a free color catalog describing Gareth Stevens' list of high-quality children's books, call 1-800-341-3569 (USA) or 1-800-461-9120 (Canada).

Library of Congress Cataloging-in-Publication Data

Langoulant, Allan.
    Everybody's different / written and illustrated by Allan Langoulant.
          p. cm.
    Summary: Rhyming text celebrates the diversity of people, what they look like, and how they live.
    ISBN 0-8368-0435-X
    [1. Stories in rhyme.] I. Title.
PZ8.3.L278Ev 1990
[E]--dc20   90-36811

North American edition published in 1990 by

Gareth Stevens Children's Books
1555 North RiverCenter Drive, Suite 201
Milwaukee, Wisconsin 53212, USA

First published in 1989 by Lothian Publishing Company Pty. Ltd., Australia.
Text and illustrations copyright © 1989 by Allan Langoulant.

Printed in the United States of America

1 2 3 4 5 6 7 8 9 96 95 94 93 92 91 90

Everybody's Different

Written and illustrated
by
Allan Langoulant

Gareth Stevens Children's Books
MILWAUKEE

The thing about people, it's perfectly plain,
is that whatever they are, they're not all the same.

Just look at them . . . see . . . they're full of surprises,
they come in such different shapes and sizes.

Some are incredibly, enormously, tall,

while others, it's true, are exceedingly small.

Black, brown, shades of red, gray, bald. and fair,

straight, curly, pigtailed, punk, Afro-styled hair.

Clothes made of leather, linen, wool, and laces;

different dress for different folk
from many different places.

11

Dressing up and clowning about
brings circus crowds much joy;

dressing up in grown-up clothes is fun for a girl and boy.

Some families have big mansions,
luxurious and gracious,

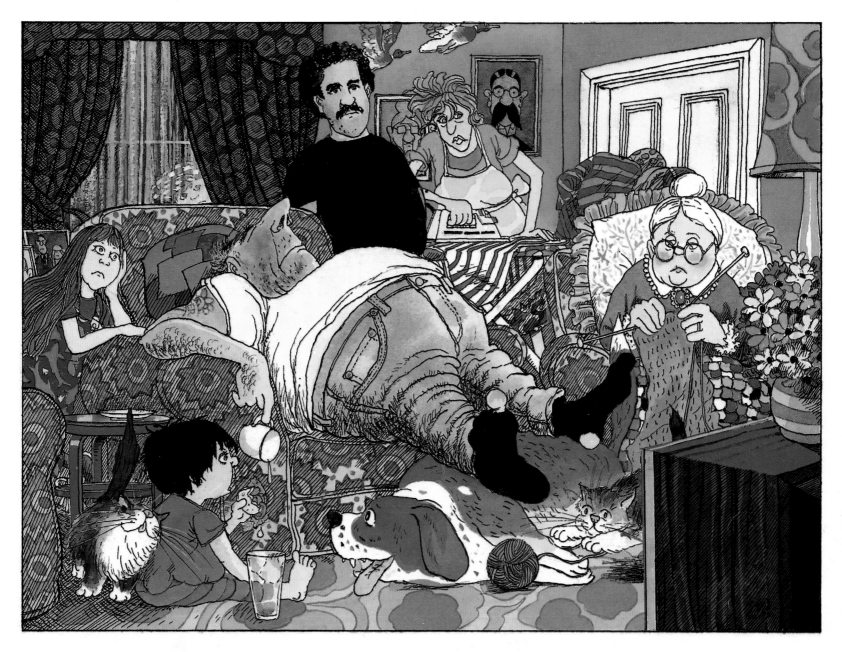

while others live in cottages, cozy but not spacious.

Some are found where the sun beats down
on the dry, parched earth below;

others live quite happily in lands of ice and snow.

Cruise ships, yachts, and pleasure craft,
anything that floats;

different people like messing about
in different kinds of boats.

19

There are many ways of moving about,
many varied ways of walking;

as many different ways as there are
different ways of talking.

Some raise their voices in chorus,
in perfect pitch and tone;

unlike some bathroom tenors who prefer to sing alone.

Rock bands play their music as loud as they can hear,

but others like their music soft and soothing to the ear.

Tackle, grab, heave, and lunge —
rough sports can be exciting,

but taking part in calmer games
is sometimes more inviting.

The thing about people, it's easy to see,

they're so very different, except for . . .

. . . my brother and me.